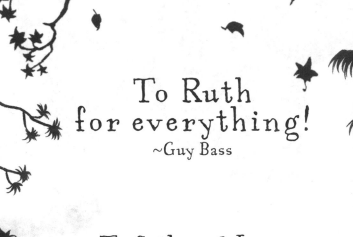

To Ruth
for everything!
~Guy Bass

To Cath and Leni
~Pete Williamson

STITCH HEAD

GUY BASS

ILLUSTRATED BY
PETE WILLIAMSON

capstone
young readers

A FOREWORD OF
WARNING

(in the form of a poem, written a long time ago by someone even older than your grandma)

Tommy Toot, upon a hill,
Tooted a smell that made him ill.
Did his best to find a loo
Within the walls of Grotteskew.
In went Tommy through the gate,
And there he met his awful fate.
So if you feel a toot a-comin',
Run back home to Grubbers Nubbin!

WELCOME TO
GRUBBERS
NUBBIN
(POPULATION 665)
YESTERYEAR

A BETTER CLASS OF FREAK

(monsters, creatures, and mad things)

It was the night that everything changed. The circus had come to Grubbers Nubbin. Or rather —

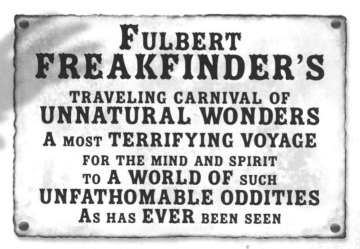

FULBERT FREAKFINDER'S
TRAVELING CARNIVAL OF
UNNATURAL WONDERS
A MOST **TERRIFYING VOYAGE**
FOR THE MIND AND SPIRIT
TO **A WORLD OF** SUCH
UNFATHOMABLE ODDITIES
AS HAS **EVER** BEEN SEEN

— had come to Grubbers Nubbin.

"Roll up! Roll up and draw near, you brave souls of Chuggers Nubbin! Witness the most mind-blowin', stomach-churnin', trouser-messin' show on Earth! Fresh from our . . . sell-out world tour!" cried fat Fulbert Freakfinder, atop his colorfully daubed horse-drawn carriage. He was handing out posters for his show to anyone who passed by. Three more curtain-covered carriages followed behind, trundle-clopping along the lamplit cobbles of the main street.

"Dare you gaze upon the impossible creatures lurkin' behind these drapes? You'll need all your nerve to behold these monsters! You'll scream! You'll gasp! You'll wet your undergarments! Behold . . . and be horrified!"

As a crowd gathered around the carriages, Freakfinder leaped down onto the cobbled street. He was distractingly short and round, with legs so stick-thin they looked as if they might buckle under his weight. He wore a battered top hat and tailcoat, which, a long time ago, might have been rather splendid. He grinned as he pulled back the curtain on the first carriage. The carriage was a cage, and inside . . .

"Preeeesenting . . . *Doctor Contortion*, the Human Knot! Watch in disbelief as he bends his body in impossible ways!" cried Freakfinder, pointing at a tall, stiff man trying desperately to get his foot behind his head.

"Stupid leg . . . bend!" mumbled Doctor Contortion to his leg. "Everyone's . . . looking!"

"Moving along . . ." grunted Freakfinder, shaking his head. "Brace your breeches for *Madame Moustache*, the woman with the well-combed face!" Freakfinder pulled back the second curtain. Inside was a burly old woman with a horse's tail glued to her chin.

"It pays the bills," said Madame Moustache.

"And prepare to have your world turned upside down by the *Topsy-Turvy Twins*!" In the third cage were two tiny, wizened men, struggling to do handstands.

"Here come the cramps!" said the men in unison, and immediately toppled over.

"Oh, cruel, cruel nature! Come closer, if your constitution can stand it! But try not to be sick on my shoes. Just sixpence a stare!" cried Freakfinder.

No one came closer.

Nor was there any screaming. Or gasping. In fact, no one so much as batted an eyelid. After a moment, the crowd carried on about their business.

Except for one untidy, wide-eyed girl . . . who started to giggle.

"Your freaks ain't scary," she chuckled. "Why, they ain't even freaks!"

"Oh, you like to laugh at a fellow down on his luck, do you? Go on, clear off, you little snot, before I set the twins on you!" snapped Freakfinder. "Oh, blow it all to smithereens! What's the point? It's the same in every town — not so much as a trickle of nervous wee from anyone. What does it take to put a peculiar fear into folks these days? I'll tell you what — I need to find me a better class of freak."

"Sorry, boss," said Doctor Contortion, now trying to get his foot to touch his chin. "We're doing our best."

"Your best has yet to be anythin' but a disappointment, Maurice," grumbled Freakfinder. "The fact is people just aren't so easy to scare any more. Well, I'm not givin' up! I've been in the horror-show business my whole life, and I'm not about to chuck it all in!"

"You were never going to scare us, anyway," said the girl, who hadn't cleared off in the slightest. "This is Grubbers Nubbin. Folks around here have got *plenty* to be scared of already."

"Is that right? And what, pray tell, are they so afraid of?" asked Freakfinder.

Suddenly, a hideous, blood-freezing, gut-churning, "GROOoWWaOOoO!" filled the air. The townsfolk shrieked and scattered in all directions, running into their houses and bolting the doors.

"*That*," said the girl, pointing up into the darkness. There was a clap of thunder, and a streak of lightning lit up the night sky. In the distance was a huge, dark castle atop a hill. Freakfinder felt a shiver run down to his toes and back up again as another heart-stopping roar came from the castle.

"Lugs and mumbles, what — what *is* that?" asked Freakfinder.

"*Monsters*," whispered the girl, her dark eyes glistening like beads in the moonlight.

"Monsters? What monsters? What are you blitherin' about?" asked Freakfinder.

"Folks say the castle's *full* of them. We hear roaring and screaming . . . and some reckon they've seen *things* atop the castle walls. *Not-human* things," replied the girl. "The whole town's *petrified* . . . but not me. I ain't scared of *nothing*."

"Arabella! Come inside this instant!" screamed an old lady, darting out of a nearby house and grabbing the girl.

"Wait! Little snot! I mean, little girl! What is that place? Who lives there?" cried Freakfinder.

"That's Castle Grotteskew! Home of Mad Professor Erasmus!" shouted the girl, as she was dragged inside. "He makes *monsters! Creatures! Crazy things!*"

"Does he now?" muttered Freakfinder . . . and an evil grin spread across his face like a disease.

THE FIRST CHAPTER

LIFE IN CASTLE GROTTESKEW

(or something like it)

Lucy, Lucy, good and true,
Went to Castle Grotteskew.
Thought she'd see what lurked inside,
But for her troubles, Lucy died.
Before she perished, she did say,
"Monsters! Creatures! Go away!"

Around eighteen minutes before *Fulbert Freakfinder's Traveling Carnival of Unnatural Wonders* trundled into Grubbers Nubbin, Mad Professor Erasmus was in his laboratory, working very hard on his latest experiment.

According to popular opinion, Mad Professor Erasmus was the maddest mad professor of all. He spent day and night in his laboratory, breathing life (or something like it) into any number of brain-meltingly strange creatures: steam-powered skulls, dog-faced cats, headless horses, flesh-eating chairs, frog-children — that sort of thing.

"Live . . . Live! Ah-ha-HA-HA! You shall be my greatest creation ever! And I really mean it this time!"

The professor always thought that his newest creation was bound to be his greatest ever. That is, until the next one came along.

As soon as he brought almost-life to a new creature, he immediately lost interest and moved on to his next peculiar project.

"More power! Live, I say!" he cried, pulling levers and administering potions.

High up in the rafters, hidden in the shadows, a tiny figure watched as the professor created almost-life for the umpteenth time.

His name was Stitch Head.

Stitch Head was the professor's very first creation. He was a strange-looking something or other — more or less human-shaped, but no bigger than a medium-sized monkey, and made up of bits, pieces, and spare parts that the professor had managed to find. His bald, round head was a patchwork of stitches, and his eyes were different colors. While the left was a small, black bead, the right was large, bright, and ice blue.

This eye was a sight to behold. It almost seemed to glow in the castle's dimly lit corners.

"Yes, yes! Now we're cooking! *More power! More!* Now a little less . . . *now more! More! MORE! Live!*" cried the professor again.

Over the years, Stitch Head had witnessed the "birth" of dozens of the professor's creations. And with each one, he was reminded how, once, he was the most important creation in the professor's life . . . that he and the professor had promised to be friends for the rest of their days.

But that was an almost-lifetime ago. Now, Stitch Head was long forgotten. He sighed as he watched this new monster open its giant, single eye for the first time.

"I have done it! I have created almost-life! Again! You are my *GREATEST CREATION EVER! YAH-AHAHA-HAHAHA!*" cackled the professor.

Stitch Head had to admit, the Creature was an impressive sight — far bigger and more imposing than anything the professor had created before. What's more, it had a near perfect balance of disgustingness and monstrousness. It flexed its two huge arms, pulling at the thick leather straps that held it in place — and wiggled a third, small arm protruding from its chest, as its master shrieked with victorious glee.

Stitch Head looked down at his tiny, mismatched hands, and felt sadder and more forgotten than ever.

"GRoOOWooOO!"

Stitch Head watched as the Creature began thrashing about, its mighty arms straining against its bonds.

"What's happening . . . ?" he whispered, staring in horror as the Creature began to *grow*. Within seconds, it had all but doubled in size. It sprouted thick fur and its huge body grew ever larger, until, with a roar, it tore itself free and leaped from the operating table.

"Oh *no*," gasped Stitch Head, tightening the straps on a small bag slung over his shoulder.

He looked up to the laboratory's great domed skylight — the moon was shining full and round in the midnight sky. "No! The *moon!*"

"GRoOOWooOO!" boomed the Creature. It swung its arms wildly, smashing the operating table to pieces and knocking the professor into a cabinet of spare brains.

"Master!" whispered Stitch Head as the cabinet collapsed on top of the professor. The Creature lumbered toward the laboratory's thick wooden door. With a single almighty lunge, it crashed through locks, bolts, and four inches of solid oak. Then it roared again and disappeared into the labyrinth of hallways.

"What a creation! My best work ever! Ah-HAHAHA!" came a cry from underneath the cabinet of brains. Stitch Head breathed a sigh of relief as the professor emerged. He dusted himself off and picked a few bits of brain out of his hair.

"Creature? Creature! Return to your master. I command it!" called the professor.

It didn't.

"I have to stop it from leaving the castle," muttered Stitch Head, his eyes unblinking with fear. He clambered silently, nimbly along the rafters, and then through a large wooden door and down a flight of winding stairs.

"Oh well — easy come, easy go!" said the professor, sifting through the brains on the floor. He held one up and gave it a good sniff. "Ah-HAHA! Perfect for my next experiment!"

THE SECOND CHAPTER

WEREWOLF EXTRACT
(Stitch Head vs. Creature)

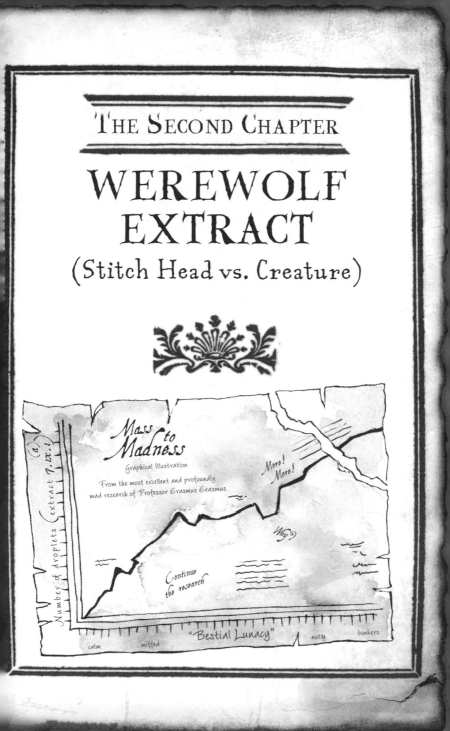

Mass to Madness
Graphical Illustration

From the most excellent and profoundly mad research of Professor Erasmus Erasmus

Number of droplets (extract 9.ix.1)

More! More!

Why?

Continue the research

"Bestial Lunacy"

calm   miffed   nutty   bonkers

"GRoOoWooOO!"

Stitch Head raced through the castle, panic stretching his stitches to breaking point. There was no doubt about it — the professor had been using Werewolf Extract in his experiments again. The full moon had made the Creature mad.

It's looking for a way out. . . . he thought. *If it makes it to the town . . .*

With every desperate step, Stitch Head imagined the professor's creation tearing through Grubbers Nubbin, trampling or squashing or eating its way through as many humans as its three stomachs could bear.

And if that were to happen, it would only be a matter of time before the townsfolk cried out for *revenge*. Not just on the Creature — but on *the professor.*

The humans would come for them. They would destroy the castle, and everything inside . . . including his master. For as long as Stitch Head could remember, it was this thought that scared the almost-life out of him.

He delved into his bag and rooted around. After a moment, he pulled out a small green bottle.

He wiped the dust from the bottle's label.

WOLF-AWAY
CURATIVE ELIXIR

For the
Treatment
of Sudden and/
or Acute
Werewolfism

Two droplets to be
taken before bedtime

Hope it's enough . . . thought Stitch Head as he followed the Creature's roars along a dozen dark, cobwebbed corridors, the fate of the professor once again in his tiny, trembling hands. How many times had he chased after one of his master's mad monsters? Dozens? Hundreds? He had lost count years ago.

Before long, Stitch Head heard the

BOOM! BOOM! BOOM!

of the Creature trying to break free.

"It's in the courtyard . . . it's trying to *smash open the Great Door,*" muttered Stitch Head as he rounded a corner and raced through the main hall. At the far end, a Creature-shaped hole had been smashed in the wall. Stitch Head nervously edged toward it and poked his head through into the moonlit courtyard.

Stitch Head *hated* being outside. Every one of the thousands of stars in the sky only reminded him how small and insignificant he was. He preferred the "comfort" of his home, deep underground in the castle's dungeons. There, in the shadows, he could almost forget that he was forgotten.

But this was the night that everything changed.

"Come on, you can *do* this . . . you *promised*," whispered Stitch Head. He took a deep breath and stepped out into the courtyard.

There, in the moonlight, was the Creature, sending its two great arms (and one small one) crashing against the Great Door that led to the world outside.

"GROWoo OW!"

As Stitch Head edged closer, he realized just how huge the Creature was — it had more power in a single nostril than he had in his whole body. The Great Door was already starting to splinter under the might of its fists. Any moment now, the Creature would be free.

Stitch Head raced through the Creature's legs. With the bottle of Wolf-Away gripped tightly in his hand, he leaped onto the Creature's foot and scrabbled up the thickest and hairiest of its two tree-trunk legs, then up its hunched back to its head. He grabbed one of the Creature's long ears as tightly as he could.

"GROOoWWaOOoO!" boomed the Creature, shaking its head like a wet dog. Stitch Head flew into the air! He reached out, grabbing one of the Creature's tusks as it roared with madness.

"AAaahhhAHHH! P-please, s-t-top!"

he cried, clinging on for dear almost-life. He felt that his stitches might shake themselves loose, or snap outright. He quickly bit the stopper off the bottle.

"Open w-wide," he whispered, and threw the bottle into the Creature's still-roaring mouth. A second later, Stitch Head lost his grip and was sent flying across the courtyard — and straight into a wall.

THE THIRD CHAPTER

THE WHOLE INSANE
MONSTROUS
RAMPAGE THING
(everything in working order)

INGREDIENTS FOR A TRULY MONSTROUS CREATION

3 parts human, 2 parts "other,"
4 gallons life-grade Cultivation Goo,
1 quart undiluted Monstrousness, 2 pecks earth,
1 peck wind, 2 pecks fire, 1 cup Vampire sweat,
1 heaped teaspoon Werewolf Extract,
4 dashes Zombie Essence, 1 sprig Deadly Nightshade,
Herbs and spices
(And just a pinch of Impossibility)

After mixing, combine carefully according to instructions.
Electrify until piping hot throughout.

Awaken!

Stitch Head had been "curing" the professor's creations for years. Since his master had started using more *unpredictable* ingredients, Stitch Head had become adept at developing potions to reverse the more monstrous aspects of the creatures' personalities. A calming potion or soothing tonic was just enough to stop the creations from escaping the castle and causing commotion down in Grubbers Nubbin. Stitch Head was quite used to risking his almost-life to keep the professor safe. Even if his master had forgotten his promise to remain loyal friends forever, Stitch Head hadn't. It was all in a day's work.

This was, however, the first time he'd been knocked unconscious.

"Owwwwww," he groaned, checking that his stitches were intact. Relieved to find he was still in one piece, Stitch Head opened his eyes. The one huge eye of the Creature stared back at him.

"*AAAH!*" screamed Stitch Head in terror. Was he about to be eaten?

"AAAH!" screamed the Creature, diving behind an enormous statue of the professor. It cowered there, trembling so hard that the castle walls began to shake.

"PLEASE don't EAT me!" screamed the Creature, looking and sounding rather smaller and less werewolf-like than before.

"Eat . . . *you?*" whispered Stitch Head. "No, I'd never . . . I wouldn't — I *couldn't*. . . ."

"Really? GREAT!" squealed the Creature. It bounded out from behind the statue and stamped toward Stitch Head with ground-shaking steps. Then it bent down until the two creations were face to face. Stitch Head closed his eyes and waited for the end.

"It's REALLY weird," continued the Creature, picking at the tiny Wolf-Away bottle lodged between two of its teeth. "One minute I definitely wanted to brutally kill everything I saw, and the next I was thinking, 'What's that funny taste in my mouth?' And then I was thinking 'GREAT! A CASTLE! I've never been in a castle before!' And then I was thinking, 'I don't even remember being ANYWHERE before.' And then I thought, 'Are bees and wasps the same thing?' And THEN I thought, 'What do clouds taste like?' And then you woke up and started screaming and I was all like, 'AAAH! MONSTER!'"

"Uh — I should really *go*," murmured Stitch Head. He bowed his head and slowly ran his fingers across his stitches before starting to slink back into the shadows. "Please remember . . . stay out of the full moon!"

"Full moon — got it! Hey, SORRY about that whole insane monstrous RAMPAGE thing, by the way!" boomed the Creature. "I SWEAR that has never happened to me before. At least I don't think so. I don't really remember anything except for the last eight minutes. Where am I? What is this place? Can fish sneeze? And why does it feel like all my bits are in the wrong order?" With two of its arms it patted the top of its head and rubbed its belly. Then it leaned down until it was nose to no-real-nose-to-speak-of with Stitch Head and let out the most almighty

BUUUURRRRRRRPP!

— right in Stitch Head's face.

Stitch Head felt himself turn slightly green as

the Creature's beastly breath stuck to him like sap.

"Everything seems to be in working order — GREAT!" said the Creature. "SO, what are we going to do now? Let's build a FORT! No, wait, let's catch SNAILS. No, wait, let's pretend we're *PIRATES!*"

"We? Oh, I'm sorry, but I . . ." began Stitch Head, edging away into the shadows again. "Please, just — forget you met me."

"FORGET you? How could I EVER forget you? Sure, I may only remember the last nine minutes, but I know a BESTEST friend when I see one!"

"Bestest what?" squeaked Stitch Head.

"Oh, totally! BESTEST friends forever! I knew we would be from the moment just after you said you weren't going to EAT me."

"No, but, wait, I mean — I don't have any . . ." began Stitch Head. He'd spent his entire almost-life avoiding the professor's creations — not because they were mind-bendingly hideous, but because every one of them was a reminder of his master's broken promise. The thought of being friends with this new Creature terrified him.

"Do you know what ELSE is weird?" continued the Creature. "We're BESTEST friends and I don't even know what your NAME is."

"My . . . name?" said Stitch Head, taken aback. It was the first time anyone had ever asked. He had never even spoken his name aloud. He took a long, deep breath and said, "S-Stitch Head . . . he called me Stitch Head."

"He did? WHO did?"

"My master — I mean, the professor."

"Well, pleased to meet you, Stitch Head!" cried the Creature. "My name's — uh . . . it's, um . . . that's WEIRD. I'm sure

I had a name a minute ago. Where did it go? Well, I'll NEVER find it in the dark, anyway. Maybe I should get a new one. What's a good name? Gordon? Graham? Gary? Gavin? Gareth? Grover? Gilbert? Gideon? Geary? Guido? Garfield?"

"Uh, I really have to —" began Stitch Head.

"Gibson? Gardner? Grayson? Gridley? Grimshaw? Galahad? Glenda? Gaynor? Gilda? Gwyneth? Gretchen? Glenys? Gabby? Gail? Gertrude?"

"Umm, I should probably —" squeaked Stitch Head.

"Gonzo? Gibbon? Girdle? Granary? Grizzly? Gremlin? Giggle? Glutton? Grindstone? Grumble? Gubbins? Goosefeather? Grapevine? Greasepaint? Gogglebox? Gumdrop? Gladrag? Gut-ache? Gravyboat? Guppy? Gobsmack?"

"Go . . ."

"Go?" mused the Creature. "That could work. It's a little SHORT, though . . ."

"No, I mean, I should — I have to go," muttered Stitch Head.

"Go? GREAT! Where are we going? I love going places!" shrieked the Creature in glee. "Is it like a tour? I LOVE a tour!"

"Umm, I don't —" began Stitch Head.

"GREAT!" cried the Creature. "Where do we start?"

A TOUR OF THE CASTLE

(monsters, ghosts, and everything in between)

High above
The castle loomed,
And while it stood
The town was doomed.

"I LOVE castles! I mean, I think I do," said the Creature, following a reluctant Stitch Head into the shadowy depths of Grotteskew. "This is DEFINITELY the most exciting thing that has happened to me EVER. Even if I can only really remember the last twenty min— AAAAH!"

The Creature froze, as a strange, inhuman shape emerged from the darkness, dragging itself into the moonlit corridor. It had a huge gray skull, with tentacles whipping out of its eye-sockets, and three metallic legs, each of which walked with a limp. It gurgled and dripped thick brown slime from its mouth as it shuffled toward them.

"MONSTER! Run, Stitch Head, RUN!" screamed the Creature.

Before Stitch Head could hide, the Creature scooped him into its third hand and lumbered as fast as it could down the corridor, smashing through yet another wall and leaving a huge, gaping Creature-shaped hole.

"Well, I never! How *very* rude," said the skull monster.

"P-p-please . . . s-s-stop!" stammered Stitch Head, as the Creature ran and smashed as if its almost-life depended on it. With its two massive arms, it punched its way into a large stone hallway. It retreated as best it could into a dark corner and clutched Stitch Head under its hairy chin.

"I totally thought that monster was going to bite off our heads and tear the flesh from our bones and EVERYTHING!" whimpered the Creature. "Do you think we lost him?"

"You're holding me *very* tightly," choked Stitch Head, his ice-blue eye bulging out of its socket as the Creature squeezed the breath from his tiny body.

"Sorry! This third arm is stronger than

it looks. Also, I'm pretty sure this is the first time I've had a third arm, but my memory's hazy . . ." said the Creature. "Okay, what are we going to — AAAH! MONSTERS! MONSTERS GALORE!"

The hallway seemed to writhe and shift as if it were alive. Slowly, more bizarre beasts began to emerge from the shadows. One after the other they came — each more impossible and terrifying than the last. Wherever Stitch Head and the Creature looked, there were monsters of every description — a six-armed slug, a giant fish with clockwork feet, a steam-powered skull, monsters, creatures, crazy things!

"We're going to be eaten! I don't WANT to be eaten! I'm only twenty-three minutes old!" screamed the Creature, squeezing Stitch Head even more tightly.

"Can't . . . breathe . . ." wheezed Stitch Head.

As the foul beasts shambled toward them, groaning and hissing, a disembodied head with hands growing out of its chin scuttled past a slime-covered chicken-dog.

"Good morning, Oliver! A fine night for skulking in the shadows, wouldn't you agree?" said the head.

"Peter, old chap! It's been forever! How's the wife?" replied the chicken-dog.

Before long, all the monsters were greeting each other as they passed by. Some were small and crudely put together, while others were huge and made up of a dozen or more hideously different parts. But despite their impossible monstrousness and stomach-wrenching ugliness, each monster was surprisingly pleasant. After its initial horror (and just a *little* bit more screaming and running), the Creature began greeting every new abomination with growing enthusiasm: "Um, hello, leggy-head-thing!" "Hello, flappy-cat-thing!" "How do you do, slimy-worm-thing!"

Before long, it was shaking appendages with everyone. These were the nicest unnatural horrors it had ever met!

"These are the nicest unnatural horrors I've ever met, Stitch Head," remarked the Creature. It looked down into its third hand.

It was empty.

Stitch Head was gone!

"Oh NO! I must have dropped him! Stitch Head? Where ARE you, Stitch Head?" cried the Creature.

It barreled through the gathered

creations, asking anyone and everyone if they had seen its lost friend.

"Stitch Head? Never heard of him! And nor have I!" said a two-headed rat-cow.

"What an odd name! He should try something more *creaturey* . . . like Lesley, or Archibald!" said a bat-winged eyeball.

"Stitch Head, Stitch Head . . . doesn't ring a bell," said a three-eyed brain on metal spider's legs. "Does this Stitch Head have any distinguishing features — anything we might remember?"

"DISTINGUISHED features? Hmm, nothing springs to mind," said the Creature, wracking its brain and scratching its chin with its third arm. "Wait!"

With a single finger from one of its mightier hands, the Creature gouged a simple sketch of Stitch Head in the hard stone floor.

The gathered creations watched with

fascination as a portrait of the stitch-faced stranger appeared.

"Those stitches in his head! Why, that's the *Ghost of Grotteskew* — I'd bet my brain on it," said the three-eyed brain-spider.

"By jingo, you're right!" said an electric-powered lizard-man. "Why, I haven't seen the ghost since I was awoken. He totally cured my vampirism!"

"The ghost? WHAT ghost?" asked the Creature.

"The Ghost of Grotteskew! He's helped dozens of us creations. On the day I was created, he appeared from the darkness and gave me a tonic for my obsessive man-eating disorder," said an oozing swamp monster. "I've been clean and non-man-eating for 1,021 days!"

"I didn't even have time to thank him for sorting out a pretty nasty case of werewolfism," added a hulking hairball with coiled claws. "'Stay out of the full moon!' he said, and then vanished into the shadows."

"Stay out of the full MOON!" repeated the Creature. "That's what he said to ME!"

"Lately, it seems that *all* the professor's creations start out bite-off-your-head bonkers — until the Ghost of Grotteskew pays them a visit," added the three-eyed brain-spider. "From the roars we heard earlier, it sounds like he cured someone just today."

The Creature was more confused than ever. Was its bestest friend a *ghost*? This strange news only made it more determined to find Stitch Head. It said its goodbyes and began making its way deeper into the castle.

"Stitch Head! Stiiiiiitch Heeeeaaaaad!" the Creature cried, as it smashed its way through the castle. (And occasionally, "MOMMY!" even though it didn't remember having a mommy.)

After several minutes of searching (and screaming), the Creature found itself alone in a wide, echoing hall. Its deafening cries rang out through the castle, threatening to shake Grotteskew from its foundations.

"Stitch Head! I only remember the last thirty-eight minutes, but in that time, you've been the BESTEST friend I've EVER had! Come back, Stitch Head, come BACK! Stitch Head!"

THE FIFTH CHAPTER

AT HOME WITH STITCH HEAD
(the Ghost of Grotteskew)

We, the beasts of Grotteskew,
Find it hard to talk to you —
The way you shriek or cry "Beware!"
We do not mean to spook or scare.
So we draw into the gloom
And hope you all will give us room.
For it is said, and it is true:
We've never meant to bother you.

Stitch Head was on the other side of the castle when he heard the Creature's cries. He had managed to wriggle free of its vice-like grip (having had a lot of practice disappearing into the many cracks and crannies in the castle's ancient walls) and had slunk back into the shadows.

But the Creature's pleas for help were as loud as its roars — and rang out to the town and beyond. They were sure to attract attention from the outside world, and that could only spell trouble for his master.

Stitch Head had no choice — he doubled back and followed the cries to a large hall. There was the Creature, preparing its loudest cry yet.

"Please . . . stop . . . *shouting*," whispered Stitch Head, emerging from the darkness.

"Stitch Head!" the Creature squealed with delight. "I FOUND you! Oh, I was SO worried, I was! Oh, Stitch Head, I thought I'd lost my BESTEST friend in the WORLD!"

"But we're not . . . I don't . . ." began Stitch Head, but then felt compelled to ask, "Why were you looking for me?"

"What do you MEAN? We're BESTEST friends forever!" replied the Creature. "I was WORRIED about you! A castle full of monsters? ANYTHING could happen! Even if they are the nicest unnatural horrors I've ever met. I'll tell you one thing for DEFINITE — ghost or NO ghost, I'm not letting you out of my sight again!"

"But I'm not . . . I mean, we're not . . . I mean . . . Oh *dear*," sighed Stitch Head.

Ten minutes later, Stitch Head had descended the last of the winding staircases to the dungeon he called home. His was the deepest, darkest, dankest corner of all the deep, dark, dank corners of Castle Grotteskew. The dungeon was so foul and unwelcoming that none of the other creations ventured there, and that was precisely the way Stitch Head liked it. The dungeon was the one place he could be truly alone . . . except for the cockroaches.

And, today, one enormous creature.

"So let me get this STRAIGHT," said the Creature, who had been talking almost non-stop the entire way. "You're not an ACTUAL ghost — everyone just THINKS you are?"

"I guess," muttered Stitch Head, as he pushed open the dungeon's thick wooden door. In fact, Stitch Head preferred that the professor's creations had come to think of him as some sort of kindly spirit, who appeared whenever a new monster threatened the peace of the castle. At least it meant they didn't come looking for him . . . until now.

"I'm CONFUSED," said the Creature, making its way inside the dungeon. It was as gross and grub-infested a room as had ever been seen, with rusting manacles and chains hanging from the ceiling. "Why hide away down here? Why stay in the SHADOWS? Everyone would love to meet you PROPERLY, and — HEY! Look at all this STUFF! I LOVE stuff!"

The Creature all but stumbled over a dozen or so dust-covered crates and chests strewn around the dungeon, filled with everything Stitch Head had collected over the years. "What's THIS for? What does THIS do? How many of THESE are there? What did I just STEP in?" it cried, having the time of its almost-life as it rummaged through the crates.

"Be *careful*," mumbled Stitch Head.

Finally, the Creature steadied itself against a table covered with potions and concoctions. Bottles and test tubes bubbled and smoked with pungent power.

"Look at all these POTIONS!" cried the Creature. It picked up a bottle and shook it vigorously until plumes of green smoke and froth bubbled up from beneath the stopper.

"*Please* . . . don't shake that! My potions, they're highly unstable!" squeaked Stitch Head, trying not to choke as the smoke filled the room.

"You MADE these?" asked the Creature, squinting in the darkness to read one of the bottles' labels. "Vampirism Reducing Ointment . . . Crazed Creature Curative . . . Anti-Man-Eating Tonic . . . Wolf-Away . . ." read the Creature aloud. "Hey, I can read! GREAT! So, what's it all for?"

"It's nothing, really," whispered Stitch Head. "A few years ago, the professor started using more *dangerous* ingredients in his experiments," he explained. "You know, Vampire blood, Essence of Evil, Werewolf extract . . . it makes his creations *monstrous* when they first awaken. Any one of them could escape into the world, or *worse* — they might hurt the professor. But with a little antidote here, a little curative there, I can keep them happy . . . keep things safe for my master, like I promised," said Stitch Head quietly.

"So THAT'S why I was rampaging! Hey, you're a GENIUS!" cried the Creature. "Have you told the PROFESSOR that you're curing his creations?"

"No, I can't . . . I just can't!" blurted Stitch Head. "He . . . he —"

KLUNG! KLUNG!

"AAAHHH! Monsters! Or ghosts! Or SOMETHING!" screeched the Creature, diving for cover behind an enormous cobweb.

"No, it's the *trumpets*," muttered Stitch

Head, hurrying to the far corner of the dungeon. In the darkness, the Creature could just make out an entire wall of what looked like large, trumpet-type horns, attached to a web of long metal pipes leading out of the dungeon. Stitch Head leaned into one of the trumpets and listened.

"Those are GREAT! What are they?" asked the Creature. It stepped out from behind the cobweb and peered inside one of the trumpets.

"I — I *made* them," replied Stitch Head. "The trumpets run all over the castle, so I can listen out for trouble, but this trumpet's *never* made a noise. I don't even remember where it leads . . . oh! Oh *no* . . . it can't be!"

KLUNG! KLUNG!

"What? What is it?" asked the Creature. Stitch Head had gone paler than ever, which was very, very pale indeed. "Where's it coming from?"

"It's happening . . . it's *happening!*" Stitch Head whimpered. "It's coming from the *Great Door.* There's *someone outside.*"

"But isn't that GREAT? The more, the merrier! We can have a PARTY!" cried the Creature.

"You don't understand — *no one* comes to the castle . . . no one's been here for a hundred years," said Stitch Head, rushing around and grabbing bottles to put into his bag. "They've *come for him.* They've come for the professor!"

THE SIXTH CHAPTER

VISITORS
(the knock at the door)

Grotteskew, Grotteskew
What do you hide?
Monsters! Creatures!
Mad things inside!

"I have to go!" cried Stitch Head. He grabbed a blanket off his bed and his potion bag and raced out of the dungeon and up the stairs.

"GREAT!" cried the Creature. "Where are we going now? I love going places!"

"No! I mean . . . you have to stay here! You can't be *seen*. None of you can. You have to stay here," said Stitch Head, looking back.

"But . . . but . . ." began the Creature. But before it could add another three buts, Stitch Head had disappeared.

"Faster," muttered Stitch Head, as he raced through the courtyard toward the Great Door on his tiny second-hand legs. Not that he had any idea what he was going to do when he got there. How could he repel an angry human mob all by himself?

Or what if someone had simply chanced upon the castle by accident? He'd need to get rid of them before they started to wonder what was inside. Either way, *he had to answer the door.*

By the time he reached the Great Door, the knocking was louder than ever, but it was still just knocking. *Would an angry mob knock?* Stitch Head wondered. *Wouldn't they try to knock the door down or climb the walls?*

He pushed a wooden crate up to the door and clambered on to it. Then he wrapped the blanket around his head to disguise his strangeness, took a deep, uneasy breath — and slid open the viewing hatch.

"Who — who's there?" he whimpered, careful to stay hidden in the shadows. A large pair of eyes peered back at him. *Human* eyes. Stitch Head gasped. It had been so long since he'd looked into a human being's eyes (while they still belonged to an actual human being), he had forgotten how *alive* they looked.

"What an unearthly pleasure it is to make your acquaintance, good sir!" said the human. As he peered through the hatch, Stitch Head could make out a fat, shabby-looking fellow in a top hat.

"Allow me to introduce myself. Fulbert Freakfinder, very much at your service. You may have heard of my Travelin' Carnival of Unnatural Wonders. Never has a more terrifyin' sight been seen by the eyes of man!"

This doesn't sound like the beginning of an attack, thought Stitch Head. *Why is he here? What does he want?*

"We've been travelin' the world, my comrades and I," continued Freakfinder, "makin' our honest fortune in the only way we know how . . . by scarin' folks witless."

"*No visitors*," whispered Stitch Head, hoping not to enrage the human.

"Aha! Mother taught you not to talk to strangers — I admire that! But you've got nothing to fear from old Fulbert," replied Freakfinder. "Now let me start by sayin' that I know people can be so *very* cruel. Why, there's even folks down in Chuggers Nubbin says there's some nutty professor makin' *monsters* in this 'ere castle. Is that so? Is there a professor in here who can make monsters?"

"My master . . ." whispered Stitch Head. "I mean, no! There's no professor, no monsters, no creatures!"

"Ha! Don't worry! Your *master's* secret is safe with me, lad," chuckled Freakfinder. "Anyway, I say one person's *monster* is another's poor, misunderstood creature, cursed by cruel fate to look just that little bit different. Wouldn't you agree?"

"No visitors," repeated Stitch Head. By now, he was pretty sure the human wasn't there to lay waste to the castle, but he still had to get rid of him, for the professor's sake. He was about to close the hatch, when:

"I ain't here to cause bother for you or your master," Freakfinder assured him. "Fact is, I'm here on *business*. Freakfinder's Carnival needs a shot in the arm — and word has it there are things inside these walls that'd scare a fellow out of his trousers. Well, let me tell you — that's music to my ears. Perhaps you could open this big door, and we could have a chat about enterprisin' opportunities."

"Open the . . . No, I can't," whispered Stitch Head, shaking his head.

The blanket slipped a little, giving Freakfinder a glimpse of his stitches. "Lugs and mumbles! What a face!" he cried.

"Go *away*," Stitch Head whispered, pulling the blanket tightly around his head.

"My most sincere apologies, my boy," Freakfinder said. "Please don't for even a moment think that I'm recoilin' in horror. No, no — in fact, I couldn't be more *impressed*. Your master must be a very clever fellow, to make someone as *extraordinary* as you! I think you could be exactly what I'm after — a better class of freak! Why, you could drag Fulbert Freakfinder's Carnival of Unnatural Wonders out of the pigsty and into the limelight. My boy, I think you could be a *star*." He pushed a single sheet of paper through the open hatch. "Here, take a look at this — it should tell you everything you need to know."

"No visitors!" said Stitch Head again, as firmly as he'd ever said anything. He grabbed the piece of paper and slammed the hatch shut.

"Wait! How about that chat? Eh? What about the enterprisin' opportunities?" cried Freakfinder. He shivered in the cold night air. "Tell you what — I'll be back, same time tomorrow, and we can talk more! You have a look at that poster in the meantime, okay?"

There was no answer.

"Any luck, boss?" asked Doctor Contortion, climbing down from Freakfinder's carriage.

"Hard to tell, Maurice. Hard to tell," replied Freakfinder as the performers gathered around. "But one thing's for certain sure — that girl in the town was *right.* There's things in this castle . . . *not-human* things. And do you know what that means?"

"You're going to start being nicer to kids?" asked Madame Moustache.

"No, you *halfwit.*" Freakfinder stroked his moustache with chubby, grubby fingers. "It means I'm going to be rich!"

THE SEVENTH CHAPTER

CREATURE COMFORTS
(a portrait of the professor as a young man)

MAD MUSING NO. 24

"The madder, the better."

From *The Occasionally Scientific Writings of Professor Erasmus Erasmus*

Stitch Head took his time getting back to the dungeon. His sewn-together head was spinning. He had often feared the day that visitors would come to Grotteskew, but he rather assumed there would be more torches and pitchforks and angry mobs screaming, "Burn the monsters!" — not a seemingly friendly fellow in a top hat.

The professor had once told him that the humans were *scared* of the castle, for they were scared of the unknown. Stitch Head assumed that as long as that fear never turned into anger, the humans would stay away. But *this* human didn't seem scared or angry.

In fact, he seemed . . . nice.

As he strolled down the winding stairs to the dungeon, Stitch Head stared at the poster in his tiny hands.

"Fulbert Freakfinder's Carnival of Unnatural Wonders . . . unfathomable oddities . . . malformed monsters . . . *behold the forgotten freaks.*"

Stitch Head looked at the blurry pictures of the so-called "forgotten freaks" and ran his fingers along one of his stitches. He had never for a second considered that there were creatures like him in the world beyond Grotteskew. What was this "carnival"? Were these "monsters" out in the open, for everyone to see? Did they have a purpose after their creation?

As he made his way down the last few steps to the dungeon, Stitch Head noticed a strange glow coming from within.

"What's that?" he muttered, stuffing the poster in his pocket and hurrying inside.

"Oh! Oh, no . . . what did you *do*?" Stitch Head whimpered, surveying the dungeon in horror.

"SURPRISE!" giggled the Creature.

The dungeon was filled to bursting with

candles — hundreds of them, of all shapes and sizes!

The whole dungeon seemed to gleam with white light, as if every single shadow had been banished for misbehaving.

"I tripped over a whole CRATE of candles when I was trying to get to the pantry," said the Creature as it licked several of its fingers. "You don't have to be in the dark any more! Isn't it the BESTEST thing you've even seen?"

"What? But no, it's too bright . . . too clean . . . too *much!*" replied Stitch Head, blowing out candles as fast as he could.

"But now you can see what you're doing!" said the Creature. "It's a total PARTY pad! All of the other creations will be knocking down the door to come here! No more HIDING!"

"But — but I don't *want* to be noticed! I don't *want* to be seen!" began Stitch Head. "I just . . . I just want to be left *alone.*"

"Look, I know you're a bit hideous and everything," noted the Creature sympathetically. "But you're NOTHING like as hideous as the OTHER hideous creatures in the castle. You REALLY don't need to hide down here."

"I'm sorry — I don't mean to . . ." began Stitch Head. "But you wouldn't understand. I don't . . . I don't want any friends. Except . . ."

"Except ME?" bellowed the Creature. "Well, obviously

we're BESTEST friends, but there's no limit on numbers!"

Stitch Head looked down at his feet — one slightly bigger than the other.

"No, except . . . my master. The professor," said Stitch Head finally. "He . . . forgot me."

"The professor?" repeated the Creature. "But he forgets EVERYONE, doesn't he? I mean, this castle's FULL of his forgotten creations. You can't take it PERSONALLY."

"But it's different!" blurted Stitch Head.

He rubbed his mismatched eyes and looked up at the Creature. "Sorry . . . it doesn't matter. It's sort of a long story, anyway . . ."

"GREAT! I *love* stories!" said the Creature. "At least, I THINK I do. Hang on, let me get comfy!" The Creature grabbed a large crate to sit on.

"Uh, I'd really rather not, if you don't —" began Stitch Head.

"READY!" boomed the Creature, flattening the crate with its monstrous bottom.

Stitch Head took a deep breath. He had never told his story to anyone. The thought of it made him feel a little more almost-alive.

"Well . . . I suppose it started with my first memory," he began. "I remember . . . waking up. The light hurt my eyes. After a moment, I saw a face smiling back at me. The professor was just a boy then. He told me that he was my master . . . that he'd *made* me. Put me together with leftovers from his father's experiments. An arm here, a leg there, an ear, an eye . . . 'Time to wake up,' he said. 'Wake up, Stitch Head.' He called me Stitch Head."

Stitch Head felt a tear well up in his

bright blue eye as the memories flooded back.

"We did everything together. My master liked to *make* things, and I would help him with his experiments. We'd play from dawn until dusk, making whatever my master could imagine — a spider with wings, a sparrow with eight legs. The hours and days and weeks passed by in a blur, and we were inseparable. We made a *promise* — to

be friends forever, no matter what. But then . . ."

"But then what?" asked the Creature.

"Then . . . the master's father decided he was ready for his son to take over the *family business* and become the next mad professor of Castle Grotteskew," continued Stitch Head. "One day, he burst into the room and said that the time for childish things was over. It was time to grow up. He banished my master from his room and shut the door . . . but I was still inside. Then I heard the key turning in the lock . . ."

"He *locked* you in? Suddenly, this doesn't sound like a very HAPPY story," whimpered the Creature nervously.

"I sat there, in front of the door, waiting for my master to come back for me. I knew he would — of *course* he would. We were best friends, after all," continued Stitch Head. "So I waited. I waited all day . . . and then all night. Dawn came and I kept waiting. I didn't even move. I just waited. Another day passed, and then another, and I — I remember thinking, *Three whole days and he hasn't come for me.* But I knew he'd come. The days turned into a week . . . and the week into a month. Soon, the weather outside grew cold. I started to forget what day it was. Long months passed. Occasionally I heard laughter, screams, roars, but still he didn't come for me. The months became years. Years and years and years. I lost count. And still I waited."

"But — but you're here! You made it out, right? Oh, tell me you made it OUT!" cried the Creature, tears stinging its eye.

"One day," replied Stitch Head, "I

was waiting when I heard an *almighty* roar. Suddenly, the door was smashed to pieces! A huge, hairy monster with a dog's head and three wooden legs burst into the room. It didn't even notice me — just kept on rampaging through the next wall. Later, I found out it was the first of the professor's truly 'mad' monsters. My master had started using dangerous ingredients to make his creations even more almost-alive."

Stitch Head looked up, his right eye gleaming in the candlelight.

"For a while I just stared at the hole in the door. Then I wiped the dust from my eyes and pulled the cobwebs off my arms and legs. Finally, I got up . . . and I walked through the doorway. I was *free*."

"YAY!" cried the Creature. "I was SO worried this was going to be a SAD story."

"I went looking for my master, but it was too late," said Stitch Head. "Forty years had passed. My master had become a fully grown mad professor. He had brought almost-life to a hundred amazing creations, all roaming around the castle . . . and I was long since forgotten. All he cared about now was his next experiment. From that moment, I hid in the shadows, only coming out to stop my master's new creations from destroying the castle — or worse."

"This is the SADDEST story I have ever heard!" bawled the Creature. "You've GOT to let the professor know you're FREE!"

GLOW IN THE DARK TONGUES FAMILY PACK

"No! No, I can't," said Stitch Head. "*This* is my almost-life now, here in the dungeon. Well, except for all of the candles."

"But you stop this castle from falling APART! You made these MAD monsters into FRIENDLY freaks! Plus, you stopped me from eating that WHOLE town. The professor couldn't cope without you."

Stitch Head sighed and shook his head. "The professor wouldn't remember me even if I was dangling in front of him."

"But how do you know unless you try? Come on, let's go and see the professor together. We can DINGLE DANGLE you right in front of his nose! He'll DEFINITELY remember you! And I'll hold your hand through the whole thing. I have three — take your pick!" offered the Creature.

"No, I can't . . . I can't!" cried Stitch Head. Memories of the years he spent waiting for his master to set him free came flooding back. He was forgotten, insignificant — and nothing was going to change that. As his mismatched eyes filled with tears, he began ushering the Creature out of the dungeon. "I'm sorry, but I don't want to see the professor! I don't want to see anyone!"

"But I want to HELP you, like you helped me! We're BESTEST friends!"

"We're — we're not friends! I don't *have* any friends! And I don't want your help! I just want to be left alone! Please, just — just go!" cried Stitch Head, and before the Creature could bellow another word, he slammed the dungeon door in its face.

Stitch Head sat in the middle of the candle-lit room and pulled out Freakfinder's poster from his pocket. Then he stared at it until every candle in the room had burned itself out.

THE EIGHTH CHAPTER

CLIMBING THE WALLS

(a chance to shine)

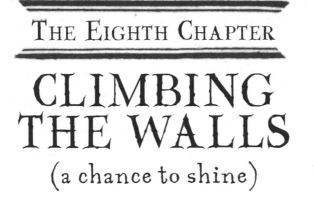

Lo! Yon Castle Grotteskew!
(I wouldn't go there if I were you.)

It wasn't long before almost-life at Grotteskew Castle settled back into a more familiar pattern. Mad Professor Erasmus was toiling on his latest creation, while the Creature had, for the moment, disappeared into the deep shadows of the castle. Perhaps it was busy bothering the other creations, or looking for a name . . . either way, the trumpets were quiet. Stitch Head did feel bad about shouting at it, but he felt much better being alone — at least things were back to normal.

Well, almost.

True to his word, Fulbert Freakfinder visited the castle at the same time every evening, knocking on the Great Door until Stitch Head answered. Each time, he would regale Stitch Head with a tale of his exciting life, traveling the world with his remarkable carnival and being welcomed with open arms (and horrified screams) at every new town. And, of course, he would politely request that Stitch Head open the Great Door. Each time, Stitch Head simply replied, "No visitors," and closed the hatch. It was almost like a game — and Stitch Head actually started to look forward to the knock at the door. With each visit, he listened to Freakfinder a little longer, and became a little more curious about the possibility of a life beyond the walls of Castle Grotteskew.

On the twenty-ninth night, however, the knock at the Great Door did not come as expected. As Stitch Head languished in the dungeon, he started to wonder if Fulbert Freakfinder had given up at last. To his surprise, he felt rather sad — and realized that for the first time in years, he no longer wanted to be left alone. He lay down on his bed and listened to the murmurs and rumbles of the trumpets. . . .

"Hold it steady, you dog-brains!"

Stitch Head sat bolt upright at the sound. It was a voice . . . and it was coming from outside the castle. He leaned into the trumpets. After a moment, he heard the voice again.

"Lugs and mumbles, I said steady! Are you trying to kill me, you muck-headed morons?"

"It's him!" said Stitch Head excitedly. "It's Fulbert Freakfinder! He came back!" He was so excited he thought he might pop a stitch.

He raced to the dungeon door, flung it open and sped up the winding stairs, following the metal pipe higher and higher until he reached one of the castle's vast towers. It wasn't until Stitch Head had braved the cold night air and stepped on to the high ramparts that he heard Freakfinder's voice once more.

"You misfit dimwits! I'm wavin' around like a snot-rag in a high wind here!"

Stitch Head followed the sound to the edge of the parapet and peered over. There, in the bright blue moonlight, he could see the top of a ladder leaning against the wall. Or rather, twelve ladders, all tied together end to end, to create one incredibly long, ridiculously wobbly ladder.

About three quarters of the way to the top was Fulbert Freakfinder, clinging on for dear life.

Far below him, an assortment of other humans were doing their best to stop the ladder from toppling over.

"Hold fast for another few seconds, you troop of talentless twits! I'm almost at the top of — AAAH! You again!" he shrieked, catching sight of the strange, stitch-faced creature above him.

Freakfinder gripped the ladder even tighter and tried to regain his composure. "I mean, AHA! *Great* to see you again, my boy! I was just — uh, passin'! Yeah, that's it! I was just passin' and thought I'd pop in and say hello!"

"I — I wasn't sure you were coming," began Stitch Head, the winter wind whipping around the castle towers. "Uh, I mean, no visitors."

"Hear me out!" cried Freakfinder, his knuckles white with fear. "All right, so you caught me! I was tryin' to sneak me way into the castle. Breakin' and enterin' is an awful crime, I know that — what can I say? Old habits die hard! But you've saved me a trip — after all, it's *you* I was looking for!"

"It — it is? Really?" said Stitch Head, trying to hide his excitement.

"Of course! Who else? The fact is . . . I just needed to get a good look at you — proper-like, all out and in the open. I'm even gladder I'm riskin' my life to talk to you! Why, you're hideous! Gloriously, wonderfully hideous!"

"I am?" said Stitch Head, running a finger over his stitches. "Is — is that good?"

"Good? It's wondrous! Why, folks would come from miles around to get a glimpse of . . ." began Freakfinder. "Well, what d'you know? I never even asked your name. What do they call you, my boy?"

"I . . . he called me Stitch Head," replied Stitch Head quietly.

"Stitch Head? Why, that's *perfect!*" cried Freakfinder, grinning with glee (and trying very hard not to look down). "I can see it now — *Stitch Head, the man-made boy!* Dare you witness the unknowable horror of a mad professor's unnatural experimentation? Who is brave enough to stare into the stitches of the creature whose head is held together with twine? Behold . . . *The Unforgettable Stitch Head!*"

"The Unforgettable Stitch Head . . ." repeated Stitch Head.

"Now look, I didn't climb this ladder just to pay you compliments, Stitch Head," continued Freakfinder. "I'm here to offer you a new life — a life beyond this castle! Why, I can make you a sensation. I can make you a star!"

"Me? But . . ." Stitch Head whispered. He looked out over Grubbers Nubbin, and beyond, to the big, wide world. "I'm —

I'm sorry, but I can't. My master . . . I promised."

"What, you mean that nutty old professor? Lugs and mumbles, what's he done for you lately? He shouldn't keep you cooped up in here, hidden away from the world! I'm talkin' about givin' you a chance to shine on the global stage!"

"I'm sorry, I really am," said Stitch Head. "But no visitors."

"You know I'm right — you've got a bright future ahead of you, my boy! You're destined for great — Wait!" Freakfinder looked on in horror as Stitch Head reached over the wall and grasped the top of the ladder. "Hang on a minute! Let's talk about this! I could make you rich! I could make you famous! I could make you—"

Stitch Head pushed . . . and the giant ladder swung backward.

"UnforgettabaAAAAAAAAAAAAAAAAAAAH!"

It was twelve minutes before Doctor
Contortion, Madame Moustache and
the Topsy-Turvy Twins found Fulbert
Freakfinder upside down in the branches
of a tree.

"Boss! You all right, boss?" cried
Madame Moustache.

"What . . . kind . . . of . . . stupid . . .
question . . . is that?" groaned Freakfinder,
spitting out a tooth.

"Hang on! We'll get you down!" cried
the Topsy-Turvy Twins in unison.

"We need a ladder! Where are we going
to find one at this hour?" asked Doctor
Contortion.

"Sometimes . . . I wonder . . . why I
keep . . . you around," grunted Freakfinder.

"Now get . . . me . . . down!
I ain't givin' up . . . without
a . . . fight. Somebody . . . find
me . . . a hot-air balloon!"

THE NINTH CHAPTER

FREAK LIKE ME

(Stitch Head's dream)

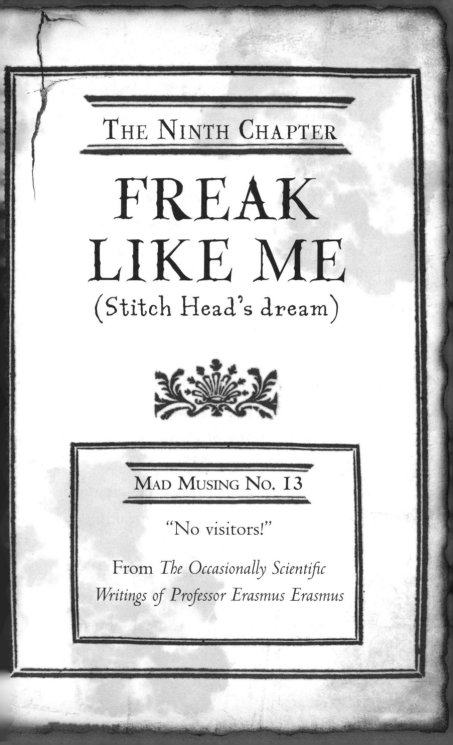

MAD MUSING No. 13

"No visitors!"

From *The Occasionally Scientific
Writings of Professor Erasmus Erasmus*

That night, as Stitch Head lay in bed, something happened that had never happened before.

He *slept*.

Stitch Head had never really needed sleep, but it made him feel more almost-alive to pretend. At night, he would lie in bed with an ear to his wall of trumpets, and listen to the chatter, clank and kerfuffle of the creatures in the castle.

But something had changed. Stitch Head no longer felt the need to listen. He no longer felt bound to the castle . . . or even to his promise to the professor. He felt free.

For the first time, Stitch Head fell into a deep sleep, and as he slept, he dreamed . . . about Fulbert Freakfinder's Carnival of Unnatural Wonders.

"Roll up! Roll up and draw near, you brave souls of Chuggers Nubbin! Witness the most mind-blowin', stomach-churnin', trouser-messin' show on Earth!" cried Freakfinder. "Behold — The Unforgettable Stitch Head!"

Stitch Head found himself atop a great carriage, drawn by ten golden horses, but with glowing candles protruding from their heads like unicorns' horns. With each tiny wave of his hand, the gathered crowds screamed in appreciative horror.

"Oh my! He's SO hideous!"

"I've never seen anything so spectacularly horrible!"

"What a monster! He's so awful! So remarkable! So memorable!"

"My eyes! My eyes!"

"The horror! The horror!"

"He's a super freak! Super freak!"

Stitch Head giggled with glee as dozens of passers-by fainted in his wake. He looked over to Fulbert Freakfinder (who, in his dream, had the head of a goat) and gave a thumbs-up. The Fulbert-goat gave a hoofs-up, and bleated happily as he counted his money. Stitch Head cast his eyes across the crowd. They held up signs saying things like:

. . . And chanted "Stitch Head! Stitch Head!" as the carriage rode past.

Stitch Head had never felt so important. It was just like Freakfinder promised — a life beyond the castle. He was free . . . and what's more, he was remembered!

He looked back and saw Castle Grotteskew on the horizon. He thought of the professor, alone and unprotected against his own creations, but the sound of the chanting became so loud that it blew away the distant castle like dry leaves. The same sound seemed to lift Stitch Head into the air. He started to fly! He soared over patchwork fields and lamplit towns, waving at passers-by, who screamed and cheered at the same time:

"HOORAYAAAAAAH!"

Soon, he was joined in the sky by the Creature, who flew alongside him waving a banner, which, for some reason, just said, "DINGLE DANGLE." As he swooped higher into the sky, Stitch Head spotted a cloud that looked like the professor. He flew toward it, but as he did, the cloud shifted in the wind, until it looked very much like Fulbert Freakfinder.

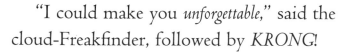

"I could make you *unforgettable,*" said the cloud-Freakfinder, followed by *KRONG!*

"Krong?" said Stitch Head, waking up.

KRONG! KRONG!

Stitch Head sat up, trying to work out which trumpet the sound was coming from. But after a moment, he realized it wasn't coming from the trumpets at all — it was a knocking at the dungeon door! *His* door! Nobody had ever knocked at his door. Had the castle been invaded in his sleep? He raced over and opened it just a crack.

There was no one there. Nothing at all, in fact, except for a piece of paper lying on the floor. Stitch Head picked it up and unfolded it.

DEAR STITCH–HED,

You hav been invited to a dingle dangle.

It'll be great!

Come to the east corridoor at midnite…wait,

do i meen the east corridoor or the west corridoor?

Anyway, see yoo there!

Yours trooly,

THE MISSTERIOUS STRANGER

It could only have come from the Creature. He hadn't seen it in almost a month. He felt a sudden pang of guilt, and wondered if it was happy with its new almost-life in the castle.

He rubbed his eyes, the dream still barrelling around his brain. He had so many questions. Could he find an almost-life beyond the castle? Would the people really clap and cheer and scream? Could he really be "The Unforgettable Stitch Head"?

And what on earth was a Dingle Dangle?

DINGLE DANGLE

(all the way down)

If you're stuck or in a tangle,
Have yourself a Dingle Dangle!

Stitch Head grabbed his bag of potions (just in case the Creature was suffering from some *other* monstrous affliction) and set out through the castle to look for it.

Upon reaching the east corridor, he found that the Creature had scribbled the words:

FOLLOW THE CLOOZ TO
THE DINGLE DANGLE! 😀 →

— and drawn a big arrow pointing to a flight of stairs (as well as a smiley face). Stitch Head followed the "clues" through the castle. They consisted of dozens of badly spelled messages scribbled in chalk all over the walls of the castle:

THIS WEY!
OVER HEAR!
YOR GETTING CLOSSER
WARMMER…WARMMER…RED HOT!
NO, WAIT, COLD! FREAZING! GO BAK THE
WEY YOU CAME! TEE HEE!

And so on. Finally, he followed a sign that read:

**NEERLY THERE! YOR RED
HOT! HONNEST!**

Up into the rafters of the professor's laboratory.

Stitch Head held his breath, gripped his potion bag tightly, and pushed open the door.

"Stitch Head, you CAME! GREAT! Over here! SHHH!" The Creature was perched on a large wooden beam, high above the professor's head. It was exactly the same place that Stitch Head had hidden to watch the birth of the Creature.

"What are you doing up here? You could fall on the professor!" said a panicking Stitch Head.

"I'm witnessing the creation of almost-life!" whispered the Creature. "Look!"

Stitch Head peered between the rafters to the laboratory below. The professor was about to bring life to his latest creation. It was covered in a white sheet, and looked even bigger than the Creature.

"He's almost finished! I forgot all about his next experiment," said Stitch Head.

"I know — isn't it GREAT? I can't WAIT to see the new something-or-other struggle into agonizing almost-life!" whispered the Creature. It pointed to a big X it had drawn on one of the rafters. "Still, while we're WAITING . . . I know! Stand here, on this spot, and you can get a better look."

"Stand there? But . . . uh, okay, but what — I mean, why?" muttered Stitch Head, edging cautiously closer to the X.

"Yes! Live . . . Ah-ha-HA-HA! Live, I say!" cried the professor, pulling levers and cackling insanely. Stitch Head suddenly felt as if nothing had changed. Here he was, watching in secret as his master tried to create almost-life. How could he have forgotten his promise always to be there — never to leave?

"By the way, REALLY sorry about, you know, UPSETTING you before," said the Creature. "I think I got a bit over-excited 'cause I'd only been ALIVE for three hours . . ."

"No, no, *I'm* sorry," replied Stitch Head. "I shouldn't have shouted at you. And it was a really nice thought, the candles. Sort of a fire risk, but—"

"GREAT! Then we're BESTEST friends again! What a relief!" said the Creature, and held up a small loop of rope. "Now let's get this tied around you."

"W-what? Tied . . . why?" asked Stitch Head.

"It's the BESTEST game!" replied the

Creature. "Have you never played DINGLE DANGLE?"

"I've never even *heard* of Dingle Dangle. What — what is it?" Stitch Head wobbled as the Creature lifted his leg and looped the rope around his foot. "Hey, what are —"

"That's 'cause I just made it up!" cried the Creature. "You'll thank me in the end, though! ALL RIGHT, time to DINGLE DANGLE!"

And it pushed Stitch Head off the rafters!

"WaaAAAAAAHH!" screamed Stitch Head as he plummeted toward the ground. He was moments from a fate easily-as-bad-if-not-exactly-the-same-as-death when the rope around his ankle pulled tight. He *KLINK*ed and *KLANK*ed as he and his bag of bottles snapped to a sudden halt.

To his horror, Stitch Head found himself

dangling helplessly just a few inches above the professor's newest creation . . . and the professor.

"Perfect! GREAT! This is definitely the BESTEST idea I ever had," giggled the Creature, holding the rope tightly with its two biggest arms.

"Please . . . pull me up!" Stitch Head mouthed to the Creature as he swung and swayed, but the Creature just waved in delight with its spare hand. In a blind panic, Stitch Head struggled to pull himself up the rope, but with his bag of potions weighing him down, he couldn't even reach his ankle. He held his breath and looked down.

He was only inches above the professor. He could see his master's spidery silver hair and his bald spot, gleaming in the lamplight. He hadn't been this close to his creator in fifty years.

Stitch Head felt his head start to spin. He couldn't let himself be seen. He couldn't face his master — not after all this time.

Could he?

He looked up and saw the Creature give a thumbs-up.

Despite himself, Stitch Head began to wonder . . . what if he had been wrong? What if he *wasn't* forgotten? What if he was *unforgettable*, as Freakfinder claimed? Perhaps there was another explanation for the professor leaving him in that room for all that time. Perhaps he had not been allowed to return, or had forgotten where his old room was, or could not find the key to the door.

What if he had longed to see his first creation all this time, but could not find him?

Perhaps it was time to be *seen*.

"Bah! Something is not right. . . . Why do you not live?" mused the professor, standing over the still-lifeless form of his new creation. "Something is missing! But what? By my father's beard, what? What have I forgotten?"

It would be so easy to call out to him, just once . . . thought Stitch Head. *But I can't . . . I can't!*

"HEY! Hey, Prof! Quick, look UP! I'm

DINGLE DANGLING here!" boomed the Creature in its roariest voice. "And P.S., my arms are getting TIRED!"

"What? No, please — *shhh!*" whispered Stitch Head, but it was too late.

The professor looked up.

Stitch Head froze. There he was, hanging just above the professor's head. He closed his eyes, not daring to catch his master's gaze.

"I — I don't believe it!" cried the professor. "Ah-ha! I knew it! Oh, *joy!* Oh, *wonder!* The answer to my prayers! Ah-ha-HA! You've been *here* all along!"

Stitch Head gasped. He opened his eyes and a beaming smile spread across his face. The professor remembered him! He was staring back at him! His bony, lizard-like face was the most wonderful thing Stitch Head had ever seen!

"Of course! Ah-HA! That's what I've

been *missing!*" he cried. He reached up to Stitch Head, and Stitch Head reached out to the professor. He felt as if he was being brought to almost-life all over again, as the professor's hand drew closer . . . and then plucked a small blue bottle from Stitch Head's bag.

"*Essence of Early Morning mixture!*" he cried, reading the bottle. "Ha-HA! Just the tonic I need to wake my *creation* with a *start*! What luck to find it dangling above my head."

Stitch Head's tiny borrowed heart *sank*. The professor had looked right past him to his bag of potions. He hadn't remembered him at all.

Stitch Head sighed the longest, saddest sigh of his almost-life, and wished more than anything that the ground would open and drag him into the darkness forever.

"Oh NO, THAT'S not good," whispered the Creature. It pulled up the rope as quickly as it could, until Stitch Head was safely back in the rafters.

"Well, that was WEIRD!" said the Creature, trying to sound cheerful. "Talk about in a world of his OWN! Uh, I mean, I'm sure he was just . . . too BUSY to, y'know . . ."

Stitch Head said nothing. He stared at the wall, his mismatched eyes glazing over.

"You know what I think?" said the Creature quickly. "We probably just caught him at a bad TIME, or something. Yeah, THAT'S it! You know what it's like — busy, busy! Things to do, monsters to make! SO many unnatural creations, SO little time. . . ."

Stitch Head nodded slowly, and looked down at his tiny hands.

"I know! We probably just need to try AGAIN!" cried the Creature, desperate to help. "There's always a better DINGLE DANGLE just around the corner! What if I drop you right on his HEAD? That'll knock some sense into him — he'll NEVER ignore you after that."

"I'm — I'm sorry," whispered Stitch Head finally. "I've got to *go*."

With that, he made his way slowly back along the rafters and out the door.

"Wait! Stitch Head! What if we FIRE you at him out of a CANNON? That could work! Stitch Head, come back!" cried the Creature . . . but Stitch Head was gone.

STITCH HEAD'S DECISION

(a lot of hot air)

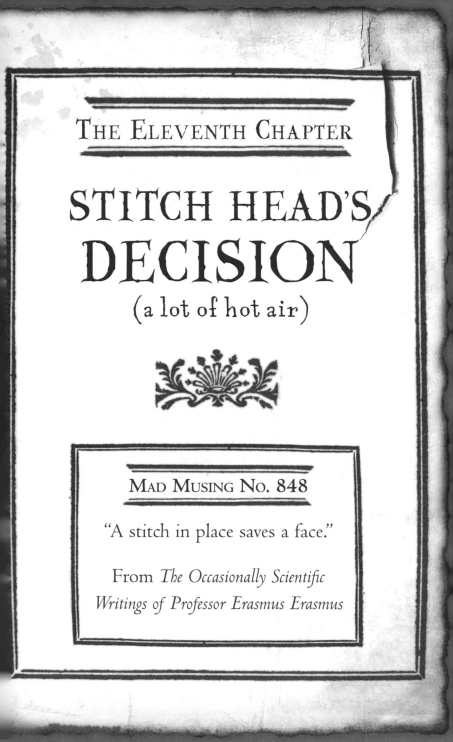

MAD MUSING No. 848

"A stitch in place saves a face."

From *The Occasionally Scientific Writings of Professor Erasmus Erasmus*

Stitch Head wandered through the castle, not knowing where he was going. He had spent practically his entire almost-life avoiding the professor, while hoping against hope that his master might remember him and come looking. Now, with the humiliation of the Dingle Dangle behind him, he felt more alone than ever. It had all been such a waste — waiting and waiting for a moment that was never going to come.

Before long, he found himself outside on the ramparts of the castle, not thinking twice about stepping into the darkening night. A new full moon sat heavily in the sky. Stitch Head breathed deeply and looked up to the stars, feeling smaller than he had ever felt. His ice-blue eye glinted with tears.

It was then he noticed something was falling from the sky. He held out his hands.

Was it snowing?

It was! It was snowing! Except . . .

It was snowing *posters*.

Stitch Head looked again. Posters were falling from the sky! Dozens of them . . . hundreds! He reached out and let one of them flutter into his hands. As he peered at it, his stomach rolled with fear and excitement — looking back at him was a picture of his own stitched-together face, and the words:

FULBERT FREAKFINDER'S
TRAVELING CARNIVAL OF
UNNATURAL WONDERS
PRESENTS
THE UNFORGETTABLE
STITCH HEAD

THE HIDEOUS MAN-MADE BOY
AN EXPERIENCE OF TERRIFYINGLY MEMORABLE PROPORTIONS
YOU'LL NEVER FORGET YOUR HORROR

It was *his* poster! A poster for The Unforgettable Stitch Head! It was as if someone had reached into his brain and borrowed it from his dream!

"Stitch Head, my dear boy!" came a familiar voice. "My wonderfully hideous friend!"

Again, Stitch Head looked up. There, floating in the night sky, he could see a large, round shape. It looked like a balloon but roared like a monster. As the vast, flying balloon-thing drew closer, he could make out a large basket beneath it. And in the basket . . .

"Fulbert Freakfinder!" cried Stitch Head.

"How about this, eh? They call it a 'hot-air balloon' — it's the only way to travel!" he laughed. "I thought it might get your attention! Speakin' of which, what do you think of my posters? I had the printers

workin' day and night
to get them ready for the
most unforgettable show
on Earth!"

"What's going ON up here?
Who IS that, Stitch Head?" cried
the Creature. It had followed Stitch
Head up to the ramparts, but dared
not step out into the light of the
full moon.

"Last chance, my boy! I can make you the most famous freak the world has ever known!" continued Freakfinder. "But I can't wait forever. I won't be coming back. This is a one-time offer! Let me in right now and I promise you I'll show you a life you've only dreamed of!"

"What's he TALKING about? You're not LEAVING, are you?" asked the Creature, still shuddering nervously.

"I — I . . ." began Stitch Head. He looked at the poster again, and then at the Creature. He remembered the professor looking past him, looking through him. He remembered the years in the professor's room, gathering dust and cobwebs, waiting, waiting for something that was never going to happen. He was never going to be remembered, not here. Not in Grotteskew. He'd had enough — of hiding, of this castle . . . of the professor. Then he remembered his dream. The cries of horrified admiration rang in his head. He looked up, his ice-blue eye glistening in the rising moonlight.

"I'm coming with you!" he cried.

———————————————

No sooner had the Creature bellowed, "Stitch Head, you CAN'T leave! We're BESTEST friends!" than Stitch Head was racing down the winding stairwells of the castle, repeating, "I'm coming with you!" until he was hoarse. The Creature tried to follow, but Stitch Head knew a dozen shortcuts to the Great Door. He quickly slipped through a crack in the wall and vanished into the shadows. He could still hear the Creature's cries as he hurried past the professor's laboratory. He didn't stop, not even as his master cried, "Live! **Live**, I say!" for the umpteenth time.

Stitch Head reached the Great Door

and hopped onto the crate. He stretched up to the Great Castle Key and turned it with all his might. The key crunched in its lock, unturned for a hundred years. Stitch Head pulled hard against the door, until he felt as if the seams in his head would come apart. Then, with a creak and crack, the door slowly began to move. It scraped and rumbled along the ground for what seemed like forever, until Stitch Head suddenly stopped pushing, and looked up.

The Great Door was open. Stitch Head peered over the horizon to the town below him, and further, to the hills beyond, and to the endless ocean, glimmering in the moonlight. None of it seemed quite as scary as before.

He took a long, deep breath, and stepped through the doorway.

For the second time in his life, he was free. But this time, he was free of the castle itself . . . free of the professor.

The hot-air balloon had just landed. Freakfinder clambered out of the basket, along with his assortment of odd-looking companions.

One of them, a tall, rigid fellow, held a large sack over his shoulder. The sack wriggled, squirmed and growled as if there was a wild dog inside.

A beaming Freakfinder strode with purpose toward Stitch Head. As he reached him, he held out his arms.

"Finally! You've done it! Well done, my boy!" cried Freakfinder, clapping his hands together in delight.

"I — I want to come with you," said Stitch Head. "I want to learn the ways of the traveling carnival, and become . . . unforgettable."

Freakfinder grinned, but it was a grin Stitch Head had never seen before.

"Take you with me? Ha!" he chuckled. "You *stupid* little creature . . . why on earth would I want to do that?"

THE TWELFTH CHAPTER

ARABELLA
(Freakfinder's true plan)

Grotteskew, how do you scare me?
Let me count the ways.
You scare me till the dark is gone
and night turns into day,
And even then I'm still
Quite simply terrified of thee.
Why, every time I look at you,
I do a little wee!

"What? I don't understand," whispered Stitch Head, as Freakfinder laughed in his face. "But you said — I mean, you told me . . ."

"I told you what? That I'd make you a *star*? Ha!" sneered Freakfinder. "Why would I want to bother with a little snot like you, when I can have an *endless supply* of monstrous freaks?"

"But, I don't understand. You — you said I was . . ." began Stitch Head, holding up one of the posters and waving it weakly.

"I said what?" snapped Freakfinder. "That you were *unforgettable*? The only unforgettable thing about you is that you gave me a way into this castle — and not before time. Do you really think I can make my fortune with you — a pint-sized ragdoll with a few stitches in his face? Lugs and mumbles, I'd as soon use them stitches to tie two cats together and call it a Siamese!"

"But — but you promised," whimpered Stitch Head, his almost-life crashing around him.

"You're missing the point," snarled Freakfinder. "I want monsters! And I want them *made to order*. See, a rude little girl told me there was a nutty professor in there who made monsters, creatures, *mad things!* You remember me askin' you if that was true, when we first met? I could see in that funny blue eye of yours that it was. I *had* to get into this castle, by hook or by crook. I tried breakin' in, but there you were to stop me! So I decided to make *you* my way in. I told you exactly what you needed to hear. It took a little time, but I knew if I made a big enough fuss of you, you'd open the door, sooner or later. And, oh! Look — here we are!"

Stitch Head glanced back at the open door. He'd been tricked! Freakfinder didn't think he was unforgettable — he never had. He just wanted the professor. Stitch Head rushed to close the Great Door.

"Oh, no, you don't!" cried Freakfinder, grabbing the tiny Stitch Head by the scruff of his neck. He threw him into the air and caught him by the leg. Stitch Head found himself dangling in the air for the second time that day. He tried to struggle free, but it was no use.

"Now, my companions and I are going to remove that professor of yours from the comfort of his castle, and engage him in more *profitable* pursuits," hissed Freakfinder. "Namely, creatin' me every kind of monstrous freak I can dream of!"

"What? He'll *never* help you!" said Stitch Head. "He doesn't experiment for money. He does it for — for the good of mad science!"

"Is that so?" growled Freakfinder. "Well,

let's just say I won't take 'No' for an answer. Oh, and just to prove it, I've made sure no one's going to get in the way of me getting what I want. See, I'm not sure what's inside these walls, but I do know I'm not mad enough to take on a castle full of *monsters!*"

Freakfinder flung Stitch Head through the air. He landed hard on the ground and skidded to a halt at the feet of the tall man carrying the writhing, growling sack. Stitch Head clambered painfully to his feet.

"What . . . what is that?" he whispered.

"Show him, Maurice," said Freakfinder. Stitch Head watched as the tall man upended his sack — and a human girl tumbled out.

"OW!" she cried, scrambling to her feet. "You mucky-rotten goats! That hurt! Wait till my grandma gets a hold of you, she'll bash your disgusting, scum-filled brains in!"

"Stitch Head, meet . . . Arabella, isn't it?" said Freakfinder as the girl dragged herself to her feet. As she dusted herself off, she spotted Stitch Head peering at her.

"What're you looking at?" she snarled. She was twice as tall as Stitch Head, and skinny, with messy blond hair — and she didn't even seem to notice Stitch Head's strange appearance. "Never seen a girl fall out of a sack before?"

"She's charmin', isn't she?" laughed Freakfinder. He grabbed the girl by the scruff of her neck and held her at arm's length as she kicked and flailed. "I . . . *borrowed* her from the good people of Chuggers Nubbin."

"It's *Grubbers* Nubbin, you pig-faced lump! Now let me go before I kick your teeth out!" snarled the girl, spitting on Freakfinder's shoe.

Stitch Head had never seen a human girl before. Were they all this angry? And what on earth did Freakfinder want with her?

"Shut it, you little snot, or it's back in the sack with you!" barked Freakfinder, shaking Arabella by the neck. "As I was sayin', I needed a way to make sure the professor's castle full of creatures was . . . dealt with. And what better way than an angry mob?"

"Angry . . . mob?" repeated Stitch Head.

"Oh, yes — quite *furious*, as it happens," grinned Freakfinder. "See, after I kidnapped miss potty-mouth here, I just happened to mention to the townsfolk that she'd been *taken* by one of Grotteskew's foul monsters . . . and dragged into the castle to her *doom*."

"You sweaty, hog-eared liar!" screamed Arabella, kicking the air wildly. "I'm going to bite off your nose!"

"Lugs and mumbles, what an uncouth child," he sighed. "But look! See there, that orange sort of glow, comin' over the hill? That is your common *angry mob*, come to wreak righteous *revenge*."

Stitch Head looked to the horizon. A fiery shimmer lit up the night sky. He could hear cries of rage carried on the wind.

Humans.

An army of them!

It was Stitch Head's worst nightmare, the moment he had always feared. The professor was doomed, and there was nothing he could do.

The people of Grubbers Nubbin were coming to destroy Castle Grotteskew.

THE THIRTEENTH CHAPTER

PLANS AND POTIONS

(Stitch Head makes a getaway)

HOW TO MAKE AN ANGRY MOB
by Fulbert Freakfinder

You will need:

Pitchforks

Torches

1 town full of people

1 small child

1 sack

1 Most Excellent Lie

"Maurice!" cried Freakfinder, landing Arabella back on her feet. "Put the girl and the ragdoll in the sack — we've got a professor to kidnap!"

"No, please, don't — don't take the master . . . I beg you!" cried Stitch Head, as he watched the fiery glow of the townsfolk's torches move over the horizon, their vengeful cries growing ever louder.

"Beg all you like," scoffed Freakfinder. "It's time to look for a new castle to creep around — this one's about to be *taken*."

All was lost. The mob would soon be at the castle. Freakfinder would snatch the professor. There was nothing he could do.

"I ain't going back in no sack!" roared Arabella — and stamped hard on Freakfinder's foot. He shrieked in pain and Arabella wasted no time in punching him hard in the stomach. Freakfinder tumbled to the ground, clutching his belly.

"Yeah! Who's laughing now, fatty fat guts?" growled Arabella.

"BRAT! Lugs and mumbles, get her!" screamed Freakfinder, writhing in pain. Arabella tried to make a run for it, but Doctor Contortion, Madame Moustache and the Topsy-Turvy Twins circled around her.

"You hog-heads couldn't even scare your own grannies! I'll take you all on!" cried Arabella, but she was still just one girl. There was no way she could stop them all.

Stitch Head looked on in horror, desperate to help. But what could he do? Suddenly, his hand chanced upon his bag of potions, still slung round his chest. He'd never even imagined using them on humans. Who knew what might happen?

Must be something I can use, he thought. He took out two bottles and read the labels.

"Creation Calming Cream? Savagery

Soothing Salve?" he whispered. "They're so . . . gentle!"

As Freakfinder's cronies closed in on Arabella, Stitch Head shook the bottles hard. Orange and yellow fumes and froth began to bubble out from the stoppers. Stitch Head gritted his teeth. . . .

"Hey!" he cried, and flung the bottles. They crashed to the ground in front of Madame Moustache, and thick plumes of bright orange-yellow smoke poured into the air.

"Hey! What's the big idea?" said Madame Moustache, as the smoke enveloped her and her cohorts. "You rotten little ragdoll! I'm going to bash your . . . your . . . braaaaiiinss . . ."

As she breathed in the bright fumes,

Madame Moustache started to sway like a ship in rough seas. After a moment, she yawned and fell beard first onto the floor, fast asleep.

"Wha-whassappening . . . ?" muttered Doctor Contortion, his eyes heavy. He fell into the Topsy-Turvy Twins, who tumbled to the ground like dominos — and immediately started snoring loudly.

"It's the smoke, you lazy lugs! He's drugged you!" snarled Freakfinder, covering his mouth with a handkerchief. "Hold your breath!"

Stitch Head did just that, and raced toward Arabella as she started to feel the effects of the fading potion cloud.

"Poke out . . . your eyes . . . fatty," she mumbled with a yawn. Stitch Head grabbed her by the bottom of her dress as she started to wobble.

"RUN!" he cried, dragging her desperately toward the castle.

"Don't order . . . me around," she slurred, tripping over her feet as they ran. "Twist your . . . nose . . ."

"You rotten little snots! Come back here!" growled Freakfinder, still clutching his handkerchief over his face. He dragged himself to his feet and gave chase.

Stitch Head pulled Arabella inside the Great Door and propped her up against the wall. He pushed hard on the door, and slowly it began to swing shut. . . .

"Not a chance!" growled Freakfinder,

jamming his foot in the doorway. He reached inside and clawed at them with his stumpy fingers. "Get back in that sack, snots!"

"Chew your . . . ears off . . . pie-face . . ." mumbled Arabella, lunging lazily at Freakfinder and biting his hand.

"YooOW! You rotten little snot!" he cried as Stitch Head grabbed Arabella again.

"Come on! Please, RUN!" cried Stitch Head, dragging her through the courtyard and into the shadows of the castle.

"Lugs and mumbles, you'd better run! If I ever see you again, that'll be the end of you!" snarled Freakfinder. With an almighty shove, he swung open the Great Door. He rubbed his hands together, and then turned to his dazed companions.

"Time to wake up, you lazy lumps! The mob's on its way, and we've got ourselves a professor to pilfer!"

AWAKENINGS AND INTRODUCTIONS

(time to take a stand)

MAD MUSING No. 121

"Mix your potion with devotion."

From *The Occasionally Scientific Writings of Professor Erasmus Erasmus*

When Stitch Head was sure Freakfinder had not followed them, he sat the all-but-asleep Arabella on the ground. He had to wake her up — but how? He rifled in his bag for something helpful. Eventually, he pulled out a small red bottle and peered at the label.

SHAKE 'N' WAKE

For the Abrupt Awakening of Creatures and Creations With an Aversion to Almost-Life

(WARNING: may cause insane rage)

"It *could* work . . ." he whispered.
"And she's pretty rageful already . . ."
He uncorked the bottle and carefully wafted it under Arabella's nose.

"AAAGH! Smash your teeth out!" screamed Arabella, wide awake and swinging her fists. She bopped Stitch Head in the side of the head and sent him skittering across the floor.

"Wait! Stop!" he cried, trying not to spill his potion as he struggled to his feet. He jammed the cork back in and checked his stitches. "How — how do you feel?" he asked.

"Like I could take on a whole army of Freakfinders!" she roared. "Where is he? I'm going to bite his toes off!"

"I don't know . . . but the Great Door is open, and the whole of Grubbers Nubbin is on its way here!" whimpered Stitch Head. "I don't know what to do!"

"Well, being a big crybaby isn't going to get us anywhere," huffed Arabella. "I'm Arabella. Now tell me your name or I'm just going to call you 'Stitch Head.'"

"It's, uh . . . it's Stitch Head. He called me Stitch Head."

"Who did?" asked Arabella.

"My master! The professor! And I betrayed him! I betrayed *everyone*," wept Stitch Head. "I wanted to be remembered, that's all. Now they're going to take the professor and burn down the castle!"

"I thought I said *no crying*," snapped Arabella, but as she watched Stitch Head fall to his knees, she placed a hand on his shoulder, and added, "Look, crazy stuff happens. It's not your fault."

"It is my fault!" sobbed Stitch Head.

"No, it isn't," said a voice from the darkness. "It's MINE."

Arabella looked around. There, in the shadows, loomed a *monster*. It was a huge beast, with one eye and three arms, and it was so terrifying that it could have stepped straight out of a nightmare. Only her natural love of scariness stopped Arabella from screaming until she dropped dead.

"Creature!" cried Stitch Head, wiping the tears from his face.

"I FOUND you! Oh, I KNEW you wouldn't leave your BESTEST friend!" said the Creature, hugging Stitch Head with two of its arms.

"Wait, this is your *friend*?" asked Arabella.

"I . . . yes, it is," replied Stitch Head.

"I'm SO sorry, Stitch Head!" howled the Creature. "I thought if I Dingle Dangled you in front of the professor, he would definitely remember you and everything would be GREAT. I didn't mean for you to run off and join the CIRCUS!"

"Oh, Creature, Freakfinder's going to destroy the castle. He's going to kidnap the professor!" cried Stitch Head. "What am I going to do?"

"I don't KNOW!" wailed the Creature. "I've only ever tried to be helpful ONCE, and it didn't go well."

"Is anyone here not a *total* crybaby?" growled Arabella. "*I'm* here now, and I'm

not going anywhere till I give Freakfinder three kicks in his big fat nose. Anyway, isn't this castle full of a hundred crazy monsters? They could scare the pants off an angry mob!"

"Um, actually, we're all a LOT less scary than we look," admitted the Creature. "There's NOTHING else to do — we have to get OUT of here!"

"No," said Stitch Head, wiping away a tear. "No more running. We have to find a way to end this. We have to face them."

"FACE them? Are you BONKERS! No WAY! They'll eat us almost-ALIVE!" cried the Creature.

"Eat us . . ." whispered Stitch Head, rifling through his bag.

He took out a round bottle filled with yellow liquid. "That's it! I think — I think I have an *idea!*"

"About time," huffed Arabella. "It had

better include a ruckus . . . or at least a rumpus."

"I don't know what EITHER of those things are," noted the Creature, "but I'd really RATHER it included HIDING in the best EVER hiding place."

"No — no more hiding," said Stitch Head firmly. "We're going to make you *scary* again."

THE FIFTEENTH CHAPTER

THE SIEGE OF CASTLE GROTTESKEW

(ways to make use of a full moon)

Let those who stay at home and pray
Be safe until their dying day.
But if you go to Grotteskew,
Monsters will be eating you!

While Stitch Head concocted his plan to stop the angry mob from taking over Castle Grotteskew, Fulbert Freakfinder had been trying in vain to wake up his sleeping henchmen. Before long, the sound of their snoring was drowned out by the cries of the approaching townsfolk.

"Lugs and mumbles, it's now or never!" grumbled Freakfinder. He grabbed Doctor Contortion's sack and hurried through the Great Door into the courtyard. "I only hope that I make it to the professor before the monsters get their claws into me . . ."

If Freakfinder had known that all of Grotteskew's "monsters" were cowering in fear, he probably wouldn't have worried. As Stitch Head, Arabella, and the Creature made their way back to the Great Door, they saw the professor's creations running around in a blind panic, looking for places to hide.

"They're coming! It's every head in a jar for itself!"

"Humans! Why did it have to be humans?"

"Quick! To the west wing!"

"No, to the east wing!"

"No, to the north wing!"

"There *is* no north wing!"

By now, the angry mob had reached the castle. There were a hundred of them, waving pitchforks, spades, axes, or flaming torches, their deafening cries demanding generous helpings of both death and destruction.

"Give me back my granddaughter, you beasties, or I'll tear off your ears and stuff 'em up your nostrils!" screeched Arabella's grandma, heading the charge. She hitched up her skirts as she marched toward the castle like the general of a mighty army. The murderous, hate-filled (but otherwise likeable) townsfolk spilled into the empty

courtyard. They roared and screamed with enough rage and madness to drown out a dozen of Mad Professor Erasmus's experiments.

"So, exactly how is this plan that DOESN'T involve hiding going to WORK, Stitch Head?" whispered the Creature, shaking with terror as it, Stitch Head, and Arabella huddled in a small chamber just off the courtyard, separated from the mob by a single wooden door.

"First, drink this," replied Stitch Head, placing the round yellow bottle into the

Creature's third hand. "That should stop things getting . . . out of hand."

"Why does everybody always try to stop things getting out of hand?" tutted Arabella.

"Tastes like GOOSEBERRIES! I THINK. Have I ever HAD gooseberries?" said the Creature, glugging down the liquid. "So, what will it do? Will it make me INVINCIBLE? 'Cause that'd be GREAT."

"Uh, not really," replied Stitch Head, "but it should stop you being *man-eating*."

"MAN-EATING? GROSS! Why would I be MAN-EATING?" said the horrified Creature.

"Because tonight is a full moon," replied Stitch Head. "And I need you to go *outside*."

"WHAT?" shrieked the Creature, terrified. "But you said I should stay OUT of the full moon — no matter WHAT. And secondly — have you not been paying

ATTENTION? There's an angry MOB outside!"

"Exactly," said Stitch Head. "Please, Creature, this is the only way. Trust me. I've *seen* you under the light of a full moon — my master made a *monster* out of you."

"I like a bit of insanity as much as the next mug," said Arabella. "But don't you think I should at least show 'em that I'm all right?"

"It's too late for that," began Stitch Head. He gritted his teeth and clenched his fists. "If we don't stop this now, it'll be the end of everything. The people of Grubbers Nubbin have to learn: *No visitors*. We have to take a stand, once and for all."

"Okay, but only 'cause you're my BESTEST friend," said the Creature gravely. It stood in front of the small wooden door, took a deep breath — and then walked straight through it.

"Um, hello . . . !" squeaked the Creature, as it nervously stepped out into the moonlit courtyard. The angry mob stopped in its tracks.

For a moment, time seemed to stand still. Then:

"Burn the monster!"

"Burn everything!"

"Except anyone we know!"

"Destroy the castle!"

"DESTROY!"

The terrified Creature wondered why it had ever listened to its bestest friend, instead of finding a nice dark corner to hide in. But as it stared up at the full moon, everything changed.

The Creature started to grow.

It began sprouting hair in all the places it didn't have hair. Long fangs sprang from its jaws, and claws stretched out from its fingers.

And then it went
MAD.

GROAWOooO!

The moon-maddened Creature's roar blew out torches, shattered windows, and sent cracks through the walls and floors of the castle. It leaped toward the mob and started smashing its way through, sending townsfolk flying in all directions. Terrified, the crowd scattered, their pitchforks and torches useless against the monstrous ferocity of such a ferocious monstrosity.

"GROOoWWaOOoO!"

"Even *I'm* a bit scared, and I'm not scared of *nothing*," whispered Arabella, as she and Stitch Head looked on. "You sure it's not going to eat my grandma?"

"It should be okay," said Stitch Head. "I gave the Creature a dose of *Anti-Man-Eating Mixture*. The minute it even *thinks* about eating anyone, it'll get a nasty bellyache."

They looked on as the Creature picked up one of the townsfolk and gave him a sniff.

"**BLEEEH!**" it cried in disgust, and threw the terrified human over its shoulder. Its inability to eat its prey only seemed to make the Creature even more savage. Within minutes, it had rampaged its way through the entire mob, which began fleeing in terror back to Grubbers Nubbin. The mad Creature roared and railed and rampaged after them.

"GROOoWoOOO!"

"Ha! Nice one, Stitch Head!" chuckled Arabella. "How'd you know all about these potions and tonics?"

"I — I had a good teacher." Stitch Head smiled. Then his eyes filled with fear. "My master! Freakfinder's gone after him!"

"Well, what are we waiting for? Lead the way — I'm in the mood for a fight," said Arabella. "Good thing I'm wearing my *kicking boots.*"

"I think we're going to need a bit more than boots," muttered Stitch Head, his mind racing. "We're going to need another *plan.*"

THE SIXTEENTH CHAPTER

SAVING THE PROFESSOR
(how to meet your maker)

MAD MUSING NO. 14

"A professor is only as mad as his next creation."

From *The Occasionally Scientific Writings of Professor Erasmus Erasmus*

Stitch Head and Arabella left the moon-mad Creature to chase after the not-so-angry mob, and raced to find the professor. Little did they know, Freakfinder had already tracked down the professor's laboratory. There was Erasmus, still struggling to awaken his newest creation, oblivious to the recent hullabaloo.

"*Live*, curse you!" he screamed, pulling yet more levers and pouring another pint of fizzing liquid into the monster's feeding tube. "By my father's lab coat, why won't you *live*?"

"Erasmus! Can I call you Erasmus? Would you prefer Professor? Prof? Profster?" cried Freakfinder, as he burst into the lab. "Lugs and mumbles, I've been lookin' all over for you."

"What is the meaning of this intrusion?" the professor hissed. "Get out of here this instant! *No visitors!*"

"I have to admit, I expected to see a few more monsters on my way here," said Freakfinder, peering at the impressive, albeit lifeless, creation lying on the operating table. "But by the sound of all that roarin', they're too busy fighting off my angry mob . . ."

"What are you *blathering* about?" screeched the professor. "I am at a most *crucial* point in my experiment! *No visitors!*"

"Visitors? Heaven forbid!" laughed Freakfinder, as he trotted down the stone stairs into the lab. "I'm not a visitor . . . I'm your new employer. You're going to make me monsters, creatures, crazy things . . . you're going to make me *rich.*"

"*Silence!*" cried the professor. "I will not be interrupted! I am about to bring almost-life into the world! If I can just work out what I've forgotten . . . *Bah!*"

"Don't worry, your crustiness, you'll have plenty of opportunity to make monsters, on *my* terms, of course," grinned Freakfinder — and threw the sack over the professor.

"Stop! I must continue my experiment!" cried Erasmus, as Freakfinder pulled the sack tight and threw him to the ground. "*Unhand* me!"

"Put a sock in it, you old lizard!" snapped Freakfinder, and began dragging the professor across the stone floor.

"Freakfinder!" came a cry. "Let him go!"

Freakfinder looked up — and up, and up. There, in the rafters, was Stitch Head, clutching a tiny red bottle in his hand.

"I was wonderin' when you'd show your sewn-up face again!" shouted Freakfinder. "Well, you're too late — the professor's comin' with me, and there's nothin' you can do about it!"

Stitch Head took off his bag of potions
and laid it on one of the wooden beams.

"You sure about this?" asked Arabella,
as she tied a piece of rope around his ankle.
"I've never even *heard* of a Dingle Dangle!"

Stitch Head nodded grimly. "It's the only plan I've got. Let's just hope this *Shake 'n' Wake* works as well as it did on you," replied Stitch Head, shuffling onto the X that the Creature had drawn days earlier. He took a deep breath and cried, "Freakfinder! This — this is your last chance! Let the professor go!"

"Go pop a stitch, you little snot!" guffawed Freakfinder. "It's over! You've lost! Forget it!"

"I'll *never* forget," whispered Stitch Head. He gripped the red bottle tightly, and jumped.

"YAAAAAAaaaAHHH!" screamed Stitch Head as he fell. He saw the ground coming up fast and closed his eyes. He suddenly wondered if he'd been wrong to trust the human girl, when the rope pulled tight. He opened his ice-blue eye to find himself dangling above the professor's new creation for the second time that day.

He stared at the bottle in his hand.

"Time to wake up," he said, and poured the *Shake 'n' Wake* potion into the monster's feeding tube. For a long moment, there was silence. Then . . .

"GRAAAGH!"

The mighty beast sat bolt upright! It was vast — twice as big as the Creature — and covered from head to toe in crocodile-like scales. It gnashed its three massive fangs and waved its six massive arms as it dragged itself to its feet and began smashing everything in sight.

"Lugs and mumbles, it's alive!" screamed Freakfinder, and made a dash for the stairs. The beast immediately fixed its mad glare upon the short, fat human, and roared again.

"DES-DESTROY!"

"WAaAH! Keep away from me, you — you freak!" screamed Freakfinder. He dropped the sack and bolted up the stairs and out of the lab, with the mighty monster lumbering after him.

26.

"Master! Professor!" cried Stitch Head. He reached up and managed to untie the rope around his ankle, which sent him falling to the floor. He scrambled to his feet and raced over to the struggling, sack-bound professor and set him free.

"Oh, my *head*! What in the name of my father's *stripy socks* is happening? I said *no visitors . . .*" he grumbled, rubbing his head and struggling to his feet.

Stitch Head looked up to Arabella. She raised her thumb and shouted, "Nice one!" as loudly as any girl has ever shouted.

Stitch Head watched the professor steady himself and rub his eyes.

He had done it. He had saved his master and rescued the castle. That was all that mattered.

"Ah-hA-HA! I knew it! I knew I could bring my creation to life!" cried the professor, surveying his wrecked laboratory.

"I've still got it, Father! I've still got the knack! Ha HA!"

Stitch Head smiled and began to retreat back into the darkness, but as he did so, he knocked the small red potion bottle, which lay, empty, upon the ground. It skittered and clinked along the floor.

Stitch Head froze. The professor looked down — and right at him! Stitch Head held his breath, but after a few seconds, the professor reached down to the bottle, and picked it up.

"*Shake 'n' Wake*," he said, reading the bottle. "Hmm . . . I don't remember adding any of that. *Genius!* I must be even better than I thought! Either that or I'm going *insane*."

Stitch Head sighed. Everything had changed, but some things, it seemed, never would. He turned away and headed toward the door.

"Stitch Head?" whispered a voice.

Stitch Head froze again. The professor's voice! Was he hearing things?

He slowly turned around. Professor Erasmus peered carefully at his very first creation as if he was searching for some old, very old, long-lost memory.

"Stitch Head," he said. "I called you Stitch Head."

He remembered.

He remembered!

Stitch Head brimmed with almost-life. It was as if all the sadness he had ever felt had been suddenly banished into the dark corners of Grotteskew, and a great weight had lifted from his tiny shoulders. He felt as light as air, as if he might float up into the rafters.

"Yes, master," he whispered. "You called me Stitch Head."

Then, a scant moment later, the professor cried, "Right! On to the next experiment!" and immediately began rummaging through a half-open drawer. "Yes, *yes! THIS* will be my *greatest* creation *ever!*"

Still, Stitch Head smiled. It was enough, for the moment, that the professor remembered him at all.

EPILOGUE

UNFORGETTABLE
(Stitch Head chooses almost-life)

MILDLY MAD MUSING No. I

"You never forget your
first creation."

From *The Diary of
Erasmus Erasmus, Age 10*

Stitch Head and Arabella talked for the rest of the night, about monsters, creatures, crazy things! Although he still thought she was distractingly scary, he couldn't help but like her. She even helped him give a calming tonic to the professor's newest monster . . . but only after it had chased Fulbert Freakfinder out of the castle. The bewildered beast quickly made friends with the other creations in the castle, and, by chance, decided to call itself "Fulbert."

What's more, Arabella refused to return to Grubbers Nubbin until the Creature had returned home, which it did, with the first light of sunrise.

"That was FUN!" cried the Creature, sitting down beside them. "One minute I was all, 'Oh NO! TOWNSFOLK!' And then I was like, 'GRAAAOWOoOO! I'm a MONSTER!' What a night! Plus, I DEFINITELY didn't EAT anyone!"

"Glad to hear it!" chuckled Arabella.

<hr />

As the sun crept through the cracks of Castle Grotteskew, Stitch Head, Arabella, and the Creature climbed up to the rafters above the professor's laboratory and watched as Erasmus began work on yet another creation.

"Suppose I'd better get back to Grubbers Nubbin," said Arabella. "Gran will probably be wondering where I am — I ain't been missing for this long since I tried to join the army."

"Come and visit ANY time!" said the Creature. "We make quite a TEAM, right? BESTEST friends FOREVER!"

"Friends . . ." repeated Stitch Head. He looked down at the professor, and remembered the years he had spent watching from a distance. Perhaps, he thought, he had spent long enough as a ghost. Perhaps it was time to try living. Or at least, *almost-living*.

"That — that sounds nice," he said.

"What a bunch of babies! We should be out there trying to find *Fat*finder to smash his face off, not sitting here getting all cuddly!" Arabella said. "Still, at least you two are completely bonkers. I *like* crazy things. The more insane, the better."

"GREAT!" cried the Creature. "So, what shall we do NOW? Wait, I know, let's play cowboys! No, wait — let's play hide-and-seek! No, wait — let's find me a NAME! What do you think? Bob? Brian? Benjamin? Benedict? Balthazar? Bill? Boris? Bertie? Badger?"

Stitch Head and Arabella began to giggle as the Creature knocked on its own head, hoping to loosen more names from its brain.

This is the almost-life, thought Stitch Head.
He no longer knew what the future held for
him, but one thing was for sure . . .
   It was going to be *unforgettable*.

First published in the United States in 2013
by Capstone Young Readers
A Capstone Imprint
1710 Roe Crest Drive
North Mankato, Minnesota 56003
www.capstonepub.com

First published by
Stripes Publishing
1 The Coda Centre, 189 Munster Road
London SW6 6AW

Text copyright © Guy Bass, 2011
Illustrations copyright © Pete Williamson, 2011

All Rights Reserved

Library of Congress Cataloging-in-Publication Data is available
on the Library of Congress website.

ISBN: 978-1-62370-007-2

Summary:
Join Stitch Head, a mad professor's forgotten creation, as he steps
out of the shadows into the adventure of an almost-lifetime.

Printed in China
092012
006936RRDS13